Noddy Saves the Pirate Ship

First published in the UK by HarperCollins Children's Books in 2010

1 3 5 7 9 10 8 6 4 2
ISBN: 978-0-00-735574-7

Printed and bound in China

Noddy Saves the Pirate Ship

HarperCollins *Children's Books*

It was a lovely, sunny day in Toyland. Noddy and his friends arrived at the harbour to play volleyball.

"Are you ready?"

Noddy asked the mermaids.

"Yes, Noddy!" replied Sparkles.
"We can't wait!" added Splash.
"Let's play the best game of volleyball, ever!"
cheered Lindy.

"Get ready.
Heeeeere it comes!"

shouted Noddy, as he hit the ball over the net.

"I've got it!" cried Splash.
"Yay!" cheered Sparkles.

Playing volleyball was so much fun. The friends laughed
as the ball went to and fro, to and fro, to and fro.

"This one's for you, Noddy!"

shouted Splash, hitting the ball high up in the air.

Just then, the pirate ship appeared.
The pirates had heard
lots of laughter and wanted
to know what was going on.

"Ahoy there, Noddy!"

the pirates shouted to their friend.
"Can we watch your game?"

"Of course you can!" replied Noddy.
"Watch how hard I can hit the ball!"

But the pirates didn't want to just watch,
they wanted to help as well!

"You don't want to do it like that," the pirates told Splash. "You want to hit it hard! You want to take aim!"

All this talking was putting the mermaids off! "We don't tell you how to sail your ship, pirates, so don't tell us how to play volleyball!" they cried.

"If you don't need us, we'll be off on our adventure," the pirates said. "We'll be back tonight."

"But how will you find your way in the dark?" Sparkles asked.

"That lighthouse will shine its light and guide us," the pirates told her.

Everyone waved as the pirate ship sailed away.

"Goodbye, pirates!"

shouted Tessie.

"Have fun on your adventure!" added Noddy.

15

The friends played
volleyball all afternoon.
Soon it was getting dark.

"Let's have one more game,"
said Noddy.

"OK. Give it your best shot!"
cheered the mermaids.

Noddy hit the ball as hard as
he could. It went higher and
higher and higher!

Smash!

The ball hit the top of the lighthouse and broke the glass. Everyone gasped as the light went out.

How would the pirates get home without the lighthouse to guide them?

Noddy fetched Whiz while Splash and Sparkles swam off to find the pirates.

"We have a problem here," said Whiz, looking at the broken light bulb. "There isn't a spare bulb!"

"But we need to fix the lighthouse before the pirates come back!" cried Lindy.

19

Out at sea, the mermaids had found the pirate ship.

"Pirates! Pirates!"

they called as loud as they could.
"The lighthouse is broken! You're going the wrong way!"

20

But the pirates didn't want to listen to them!

"Are you trying to tell us how to sail our ship?" the pirates asked. "You wouldn't listen to us about volleyball, so we're not going to listen to you!"

"Arrr!"

the pirates cried, as they sailed away.

Back at the lighthouse, Noddy had
come up with a big Noddy plan!

"We'll use Whiz's torch to guide the pirates back,"
he told Lindy.
"If you use your magic to make it bigger,
the light will be bright enough!"

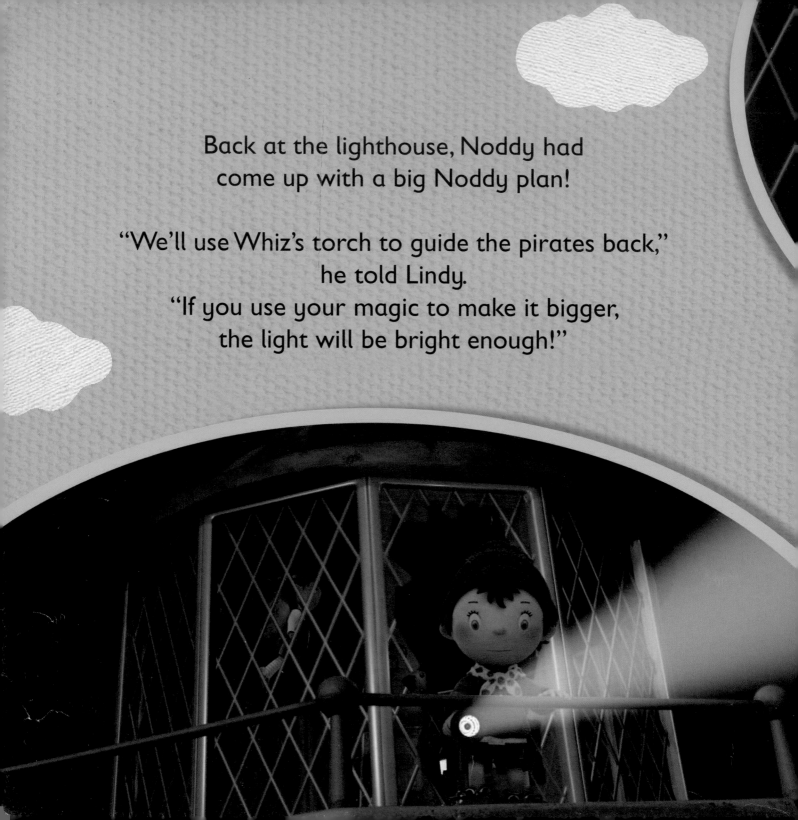

"Good idea, Noddy!" said Lindy,
as she sprinkled magic dust
on the torch.

23

As the torch got bigger and bigger
and bigger, the light got brighter
and brighter and brighter!

"It's working!"

cheered Noddy.

On the ship, the pirates spotted the light.

"Look, the lighthouse!"

they cried.
"We're heading the wrong way!
Turn around!"

The friends cheered as the pirate ship
turned the right way.

"Hurray! Hurray!
Hurray!"

"We did it!"

cried Noddy.
"The pirates are safely
away from the shore!"

Noddy, Tessie, Lindy and Whiz hurried
down to the pirate ship.

"A-hoy there, come aboard!"

the pirates cried. "Thanks for saving us!"

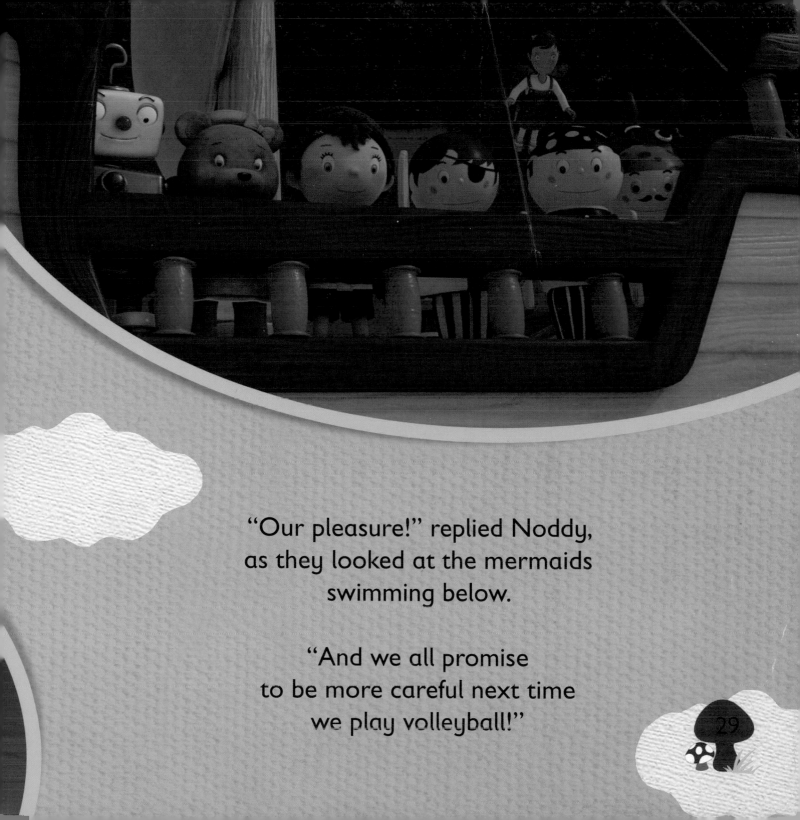

"Our pleasure!" replied Noddy,
as they looked at the mermaids
swimming below.

"And we all promise
to be more careful next time
we play volleyball!"

29

NODDY
IN TOYLAND ®

**Look out for more
Noddy in Toyland books!**

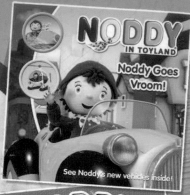

NODDY
IN TOYLAND
Noddy Goes Vroom!

See Noddy's new vehicles inside!

NODDY
IN TOYLAND
Noddy and the Pirates

NODDY
IN TOYLAND
Hide-and-Seek Fun

NODDY
IN TOYLAND
The Magic Watering Can

NODDY
IN TOYLAND
A Very Special Birthday

NODDY
IN TOYLAND
The Magic Paintbrush